Wendy and the Dog Wash

The Sound of W

by Joanne Meier and Cecilia Minden • illustrated by Bob Ostrom

The Child's World®

Published by The Child's World®
1980 Lookout Drive
Mankato, MN 56003-1705
800-599-READ
www.childsworld.com

The Child's World®: Mary Berendes, Publishing Director
The Design Lab: Design and page production

Library of Congress Cataloging-in-Publication Data
Meier, Joanne D.
  Wendy and the dog wash : the sound of W /
by Joanne Meier and Cecilia Minden ; illustrated by
Bob Ostrom.
    p. cm.
  ISBN 978-1-60253-421-6 (library bound : alk. paper)
  1. English language—Consonants—Juvenile literature.
  2. English language—Phonetics—Juvenile literature. 3.
Reading—Phonetic method—Juvenile literature. I. Minden,
Cecilia. II. Ostrom, Bob. III. Title.
  PE1159.M48 2010
  [E]—dc22   2010005610

Printed in the United States of America in Mankato, MN.
July 2010
F11538

NOTE TO PARENTS AND EDUCATORS:

The Child's World® has created this series with the goal of exposing children to engaging stories and illustrations that assist in phonics development. The books in the series will help children learn the relationships between the letters of written language and the individual sounds of spoken language. This contact helps children learn to use these relationships to read and write words.

The books in this series follow a similar format. An introductory page, to be read by an adult, introduces the child to the phonics feature, or sound, that will be highlighted in the book. Read this page to the child, stressing the phonic feature. Help the student learn how to form the sound with her mouth. The story and engaging illustrations follow the introduction. At the end of the story, word lists categorize the feature words into their phonic elements.

Each book in this series has been carefully written to meet specific readability requirements. Close attention has been paid to elements such as word count, sentence length, and vocabulary. Readability formulas measure the ease with which the text can be read and understood. Each book in this series has been analyzed using the Spache readability formula.

Reading research suggests that systematic phonics instruction can greatly improve students' word recognition, spelling, and comprehension skills. This series assists in the teaching of phonics by providing students with important opportunities to apply their knowledge of phonics as they read words, sentences, and text.

This is the letter w.

In this book, you will read words
that have the **w** sound as in:
wash, wet, water, and *work.*

Wendy has a big job.
She has to wash her
dog, Wags.

First, Wendy gets Wags all
wet. She uses warm water.

Wendy washes Wags.

Wags likes the warm water.

Wendy wishes Wags would stand still. This is hard work!

Wendy gets the soap.

She washes the dog well.

Wendy uses more water.

She makes sure the water

is warm.

Wendy is done.

Wags is clean and wet!

Wendy wants to dry Wags.

She gets a warm towel.

Oh no! Wags shakes and shakes. Now Wags and Wendy are both wet!

Fun Facts

Water makes up most of our planet and plays a very important part in our lives. If you think of Earth as a giant pie with ten pieces, eight of those pieces would represent the portion of Earth's surface that is made up of water. Of those eight pieces, less than one would represent the amount of water that is safe for drinking. The rest is seawater or water that is frozen in glaciers.

Perhaps you don't have a job right now, but you probably would if you lived in the 1800s. Children worked in mines, factories, farms, and stores. They picked cotton, shined shoes, sold newspapers, canned fish, made clothes, and wove fabric. They usually worked twelve hours a day, seven days a week!

Activity

Performing an Experiment with Water
Fill a glass with water until it is completely full. Next, drop one coin into the water. Slowly add another, and then another. You will probably start to notice that the surface of the water becomes more and more rounded. The water is allowing the surface to stretch before it breaks and the water overflows. See how many coins it takes before the water overflows.

To Learn More

Books
About the Sound of W
Moncure, Jane Belk. *My "w" Sound Box®*. Mankato, MN: The Child's World, 2009.

About Water
Dorros, Arthur. *Follow the Water from Brook to Ocean*. New York: HarperTrophy, 1993.
Green, Jen, and Mike Gordon (illustrator). *Why Should I Save Water?* Hauppauge, NY: Barron's Educational Series, 2005.
Kerley, Barbara. *A Cool Drink of Water*. Washington, DC: National Geographic Society, 2006.

About Work
Johnson, D. B. *Henry Works*. Boston: Houghton Mifflin, 2004.
Morris, Ann. *Work*. New York: Lothrop, Lee & Shepard Books, 1998.
Nelson, Robin. *Working Then and Now*. Minneapolis, MN: Lerner Pub., 2008.

Web Sites
Visit our home page for lots of links about the Sound of W:

childsworld.com/links

Note to Parents, Teachers, and Librarians: We routinely check our Web links to make sure they're safe, active sites—so encourage your readers to check them out!

W Feature Words

Proper Names
Wags
Wendy

Feature Words in Initial Position
warm
wash
wash
water
well
wet
wish
work
would

About the Authors

Joanne Meier, PhD, has worked as an elementary school teacher, university professor, and researcher. She earned her BA in early childhood education from the University of South Carolina, and her MEd and PhD in education from the University of Virginia. She currently works as a literacy consultant for schools and private organizations. Joanne lives in Virginia with her husband Eric, daughters Kella and Erin, two cats, and a gerbil.

Cecilia Minden, PhD, is the former director of the Language and Literacy Program at the Harvard Graduate School of Education. She is now a reading consultant for school and library publications. She earned her PhD in reading education from the University of Virginia. Cecilia and her husband, Dave Cupp, live outside Chapel Hill, North Carolina. They enjoy sharing their love of reading with their grandchildren, Chelsea and Qadir.

About the Illustrator

Bob Ostrom has been illustrating children's books for nearly twenty years. A graduate of the New England School of Art & Design at Suffolk University, Bob has worked for such companies as Disney, Nickelodeon, and Cartoon Network. He lives in North Carolina with his wife Melissa and three children, Will, Charlie, and Mae.